Love Potion No. 69

VALERIE PEPPER

For the witchy girls with scarves on their lamps and too many candles to count.

And for the girls who wish a little magic existed in the world... and the girls who know it's already here.

CLEMENTINE

*O*NCE UPON A time, there was a princess...
   Nope. Not accurate.
   Once upon a time, there was a girl...
Scratch that. Everyone treats me like I'm far younger than my twenty-seven years, so let's try that again.

I hold the glass jar up, the sun's light refracting through the clear liquid, and hold my breath as I slowly pour the Elysian Blossom essence in.

"Please don't cloud, don't cloud, don't...son of a biscuit eater!" Sighing, I set the jar down, put the vial of essence back in the refrigerator, and grab my notebook and pencil. Love potion number 68, bust.

Once upon a time, there was a botanist who was tired of her sisters treating her like a baby, so she decided to recreate the famous love potion her family was once known for. Except the potion was never written down, and the botanist's mother only remembered how it smelled instead of what was in it, which was supremely unhelpful. So the botanist toiled day after day in her greenhouse laboratory, her only exposure to sunlight the rays that came through the glass surrounding her, and definitely no prince to speak of.

Better. Except when would I actually have time for a prince? Also, it's the twenty-first century in America, and unless I'm aiming for the British guy who's living on the West Coast with his gorgeous wife and family after having told the crown to shove it, then no prince for me.

I finish my notes, then pull my hair into a bun and secure it with a pencil right as my sister Magnolia comes into the greenhouse.

"Hey, Clemmy-clem-Clementine!" she calls, her voice as bright as the sun outside. "Figured I'd find you in here." She holds out a mug of tea as she approaches, and I take it gratefully.

"Thank you." I inhale the aroma before sipping, because as grateful as I am for the tea, I also know my family's tendencies when it comes to tea. Granted, Magnolia is the second-oldest of us and generally behaves herself, but there's a lot of things growing on our land that can be put to mischievous use. All I smell is lemon and verbena, so I'm going to assume it's safe. After a small sip, I grin and take a larger drink.

She quirks a dark brow at me. "So suspicious," she chides.

"Do you blame me?" I ask, taking another deep gulp. It's the perfect temperature, and none of us have figured out how to keep a ceramic cup heated, so I need to drink it now.

Magnolia laughs. "No, I don't. But I'm here with a favor."

I sigh. "I swear, if you're here to ask me to call Hazel and beg her to come home for a visit—"

"No, not that," she says. "Not today, anyway."

"Then what?"

She hesitates, and instantly I'm on edge.

"Mags, out with it. You're freaking me out. None of you ever ask for a favor, unless it's to help play a trick on some-one, and I'm really busy—"

"Could you come talk to my class on Tuesday?"

I stop mid-sentence, clamping my mouth shut and squinting at her through my glasses. "I'm sorry. Did you just ask me to come speak to your class?"

She nods, a hopeful look in her amber eyes. "I thought I'd let them see what a career that uses chemistry looks like."

I sigh. "You know how much I hated high school. Why would I willingly go back there?"

"Because your favorite sister is begging you? Because I'm the only one who doesn't give you shit on a constant basis? Because—"

"Fine," I cut her off, knowing it's better to give in than endure the constant stream of reasons she'll come up with. "I'll do it. You owe me."

She jumps up and down and rushes me, wrapping me in a crushing hug and saying "thank you" on repeat. I manage to save the tea, but only barely. When she lets me go, I finish it and hand the cup back to her.

"You need to send me a calendar appointment. Otherwise, I can't be held responsible for missing it," I say.

She flashes me a wide smile. "You got it." Then she assesses my work station. "Now that I've gotten the boring stuff out of the way, how's it going?"

I let out a frustrated groan. "Horribly. I thought I was onto something, but the last batch clouded as soon as I put the Elysian Blossom essence in."

Magnolia's eyes widen. "You're using *Elysian Blossom*?"

I smile. "Yep."

She frowns. "But—but it only blooms once every hundred years. It's extremely rare. Our family is the only one that even has seeds, and you know how important it is to us, Clementine."

I cross my arms, instantly on the defensive. "Quit using your teacher voice on me, Mags."

She's not fazed. "Clearly, someone has to. Does Mom know?"

I grind my teeth. This is exactly why I don't like my family to come in here. Never mind that I'm a grown woman with a degree and plenty of common sense. All they see are the messes I made as a little girl with insatiable curiosity. The burn on my right hand and arm, the color of an over-ripe strawberry against my olive skin, doesn't let them forget, either.

"Well? Does she?" Magnolia prompts.

"She doesn't, and she doesn't need to," I shoot back.

Magnolia barks a laugh. "You're hilarious. Mom will kill you."

She won't. But Mags doesn't know that. "Could you for once, just *once*, pretend that I might actually know what I'm doing?" I keep my voice calm and even, despite preferring to screech at her. "Pretend, for just a moment, that I have been doing this research for five years. Pretend that I'm the one who tends to our land. Pretend that I might have figured out a way to force the flower to bloom when I want it to, and that I've managed to capture its essence in a way that doesn't harm it."

She shakes her head. "You're begging for trouble."

"I'm really not. I know what I'm doing," I repeat. And if Mom bothered to pay any attention to me, or to come knocking on the greenhouse door, I'd have happily shown her what I was doing, the progress I was making.

My phone pings from beneath my notebook, and we both turn in its direction.

"Who's that?" Magnolia asks.

I roll my eyes. "I don't know. I haven't looked yet. Also, it's none of your business."

"Since when has that stopped me?" she asks, angling her

body to look at the screen with me. Then she snorts. "Who is 'Entitled Canadian Asshole'?"

I smash the phone against my chest. "No one."

"That doesn't seem to be the case."

I consider her eager eyes and the way they betray her carefully presented patience. It wouldn't be a bad idea to have a sister on my side, and honestly, if I could choose the sister to go to battle with, it's always going to be Mags. She is the one who gives me the least shit, and in my family, that's saying something. "It's this man, Quinton Henry."

She gasps. "The perfume prince of Canada?"

The effort it takes for me to not roll my eyes at that ridiculous nickname should win me an award. "Yes."

"What does he want?"

"Christ, Mags—why don't you stop talking and I'll *tell* you?" I huff.

Properly chastised for a whole two seconds, she nods.

I continue. "He wants to buy Elysian Blossom seeds."

Immediately, every part of her goes on high alert. "Absolutely not."

I smile wryly. "Yeah, no shit. And that's what I've continued to tell him, but it's not sinking in."

"So what's he saying now?"

I hold the phone so we can read it together.

ENTITLED CANADIAN

> I'm certain I can convince you. Please send me your address. I'll be there tomorrow.

Magnolia sucks in a breath. "He's coming here? To Sacred River?"

Forcing down the spike of anger at the man's audacity, I answer. "It would appear so."

"Does he have any clue what he's walking into?"

"Not even remotely."

She chuckles. "Well. Guess we'll have to show the perfume prince of Canada a good time."

QUINTON

I'VE GOT TO admit, it's nice to be on the receiving end
of my parents' approval for once. And a little discon-
certing, if I'm being honest. I've grown so used to their
constant disappointment over the years that to have them
actually smiling at me without cameras around feels...odd.
Like a coat that's gotten too tight.

Mom—CEO of Scentsual Enterprises Angela Henry to the
rest of the world—looks positively giddy as she walks around
the massive desk in her corner office. "You're really going
down there?" she asks.

Dad puts his hand on her shoulder, as if to keep her from
floating away on a cloud of enthusiasm. "I think what your
mother is saying is that she's very proud of the way you're
stepping up and helping the family." Then he widens his
nostrils and sniffs as he leans towards me. "You should wear
Winter when you meet the woman, however. It works better
with your body's chemistry."

I grin, already more at ease now that Dad's given me one
of his classic unsolicited opinions. He's not wrong about the
scent—the man's olfactory system is quite literally insured

for ten million dollars—but it doesn't mean I have to use it every day. In fact, today's smell is brought to you by eau de Quinton. In other words, nothing but the soap I used in the gym's shower after my workout. "Sure thing, Dad."

"You are not to take no for an answer." My grandmother's soft voice belies the power she holds. Dressed in one of her standard cashmere sweater sets and slacks, she's perched on the edge of the cream-colored couch that overlooks the small downtown of Coal's Lake. She's been in this corner office longer than either of my parents have been alive, and while she may have "retired" a decade ago, the old woman has taken more than a passing interest in our family's 150th perfume empire anniversary.

"Understood, Grand-mère," I murmur. Because what else am I going to say? The woman will string me up by my balls if I do anything else.

"Notwithstanding my shock at you having the where-withal to find evidence that the Elysian Blossom still exists," she continues, her watery brown eyes sharp as ever as they appraise me, "something tells me that the family you're trying to procure it from will be a bit, shall we say, protective."

I manage to contain my snort of derision. I have never been told no. Not when I was a kid, not those years in college with Axl and Gabriel when no one bothered to put two and two together and realize who I was, and certainly not as an adult. I'm smart, I'm charming as fuck, and honestly? I'm sexy as hell. This Clementine Rowan won't know what hit her.

"Quinton Henry." Grand-mère's voice, full of reproach, cuts through my moment of self-love.

"Yes, ma'am," I say. "But all due respect, I think I'll be able to get the family to see reason." Because I refuse to think about what will happen if they don't.

Grand-mère gives a haughty sniff that tells me what she thinks of my confidence, but she's not seen me in action.

To be fair, *no one* in my family has seen me in action, because I stayed out of the family business as long as possible. But I'm the last one standing, and although I delayed the inevitable, I finally joined the company a few years ago when I turned twenty-four. Grand-mère has always been extremely outspoken my entire life about my involvement in the family business, both for the good of our family and the town. So I joined, but it took another year before I really got good and interested. Now? I'm all in. And nothing will stop me from getting that flower essence for us.

"I believe in you, son," Dad says, his wide smile and deep brown eyes full of love.

"You'll call us when it's done?" Mom asks.

I nod, squashing the tiniest inkling of doubt that keeps trying to take root deep in my chest. "Of course."

After a few more pleasantries, I kiss them goodbye and drive to my tiny apartment a few miles away. My family has been in Coal's Lake for as long as the company's been around, and while a part of me would love to escape the confines of it and the easy access it gives the paparazzi, our family is too loyal to the town to leave. People who looked like us—Black people—weren't generally given a lot of chances back in the late 1800s in Canada, but this small town didn't care what we looked like. They cared that my great-great-grandfather had enough money to start a business, and what began as a small perfumery found incredible success thanks to one specific scent.

The story goes that a woman from Sacred River, a tiny town in the southern United States, visited the area and needed a place to stay for a few days. My great-great-grandfather and great-great-grandmother opened their house to her, and as thanks, the woman left them a bottle of Elysian

Blossom essence. The flower is extremely rare and was known to grow only in Sacred River. Being the type of people to never let a good thing go to waste, the enterprising perfumers used the essence in a scent they called, somewhat on the nose, *Blossoming Elysian*. Family lore says that the bottle never seemed to empty for one hundred years, and we manufactured the scent and sold it around the world, trying and failing the entire time to recreate the essence in the lab. We stopped production when the bottle ran out, but by then our company was a household name, and thanks to my parents' antics when they were younger, it also put a spotlight on the family itself.

When I finally stepped into the business, the paparazzi had a field day with me. Suddenly I was the "prince of perfume" and my every movement was watched. While they've chilled out a bit, I still get followed every now and then. It's second nature to look around for one of them before unlocking the door to my townhouse, stepping inside, and going upstairs to pack.

With our 150th anniversary coming up next year, my job is to recreate the famous scent that's been out of production for fifty years. No pressure or anything. Dad's nose is blind to the particular odor of Elysian Blossom, which has always seemed highly improbable, but he and Grand-mère insist he's unable to smell the flower's essence in the one remaining bottle of Blossoming Elysian perfume we have.

Guess who can?

Your boy Q.

And yet, there's something about the scent that I can't quite put my finger on. It makes me have this nostalgic yearning for something or someone, and I'm certain that the Elysian Blossom is responsible for that precise feeling, that indecipherable pull in the chest. I've read the old editorials in fashion magazines and old newspapers bemoaning the perfume's disappearance, read about the near-riots at department stores when word got out that whatever was on the shelves was all that was left, and I have no doubt the world wants it again.

So if I can bring that scent back to life, I'm not only saving my family's legacy, I'm taking us from millionaires to billionaires. Not bad by a former slacker gamer whose friends figured he'd remain a lazy bachelor for the rest of his life.

I pull out my phone and send a text to the delightfully stubborn Clementine Rowan, informing her of my arrival tomorrow and requesting her address. I'll meet her face to face and convince her to sell me the seeds so we can grow the flowers in Coal's Lake.

Piece of cake.

CLEMENTINE

I'M UP WITH the birds like always. After making a cup of my oldest sister Aspen's special blend of morning-time tea, I curl up in the wicker loveseat on the back porch and watch the sun rise over the family willow tree in the distance. Pink is always the first to arrive in the winter, shooting streaks of brightness into the sky and demanding to be seen before all the other colors, and I whistle a hello to the color before I take my first sip of tea.

A pair of cardinals tweet back from their perch in the blueberry bush that runs alongside the house, and I grin. We trade a few more whistles, and while none of us is truly certain of what the other is saying, I'm convinced that today is going to be a good day. I felt it when I woke up, and my feathered friends confirm it.

The kitchen light comes on behind me, the warm yellow spilling onto the porch around me and announcing the next person's awakening. I send a question into the atmosphere, and I get my answer: Mom. The pipes squeak as she pours her morning glass of water, and the floorboards' creaking makes its way outside, as well. I love our house. It's big and messy and loud, kind of like our family, and I wouldn't have it any other way. We're all still here: Mom, Aspen, Magnolia, Willow, Juniper and Jasmine, and me. The only one missing is Hazel, who's doing her residency in Boston and who my sisters are convinced will eventually return home, but I don't think she will. She's never believed in our gifts, explaining everything away with hard-headed logic and deciding to become a medical doctor to wield her preternatural ability to understand the body. She doesn't need the training, but I stopped trying to convince her when I was five.

Just as I finish my tea, Mom arrives with the teapot. She smiles and pours me another round, then tucks herself beside me under the cozy blanket with her own cup. She bends her knees up, curling into a ball as she leans into me. "Good morning, my youngest."

I tilt my head to her, snuggling back. "Good morning, oldest."

She swats me as she softly laughs. "Watch it, you." Her bright blue eyes miss nothing as she scans me, and I swear she can see under the blanket. I know all mothers seem to see everything, but Daphne Rowan takes mothering to a whole different level. She squints. "What aren't you telling me?"

I huff a laugh. "Nothing."

She shakes her head and raises her eyebrows. "You and I both know that's not true," she prompts.

She's right, of course, but I decide to go with the easier tale. "There's a man coming today."

"He wants something." It's not exactly a question.

I sip the tea. It's not Aspen's blend, but Mom's, and while she's never revealed the one ingredient that none of us can figure out, I can guarantee it's a truth serum. And it's cute how she still thinks it works on me, when it was literally the first thing I created an antidote for. I was six.

"Don't they always?" I ask. Because it's true. Never have I met a man who wasn't after one thing or another: my body, my recipes, my sisters.

Mom makes a noncommittal grunt.

I take another sip. "He wants to buy Elysian Blossom seeds," I finally say. "His family had a bottle of the essence and used it to make perfume, but the bottle ran out."

Mom closes her eyes. "The Henrys. Coal's Lake."

"Yes."

Before she can say anything else, Aspen strides outside, her deep blonde hair waving in the breeze. "You getting a ride with me to the shop?"

"Of course," Mom says, unfolding herself and rising. "I have a delivery of books set to come in. They'll be there—"

"At eleven thirteen," Aspen finishes, already turning to go back inside. "I know. Mondays are when we get all our shipments."

Mom follows Aspen inside, but pauses at the door to look back at me. The sun's rays frame her pixie face and graying hair as she says, "You know what to do, Clementine."

I nod and drain the tea. Above me, a clutch of starlings squawk as a fat black cat twirls his way around the deck furniture. His green eyes are far from innocent as he blinks up at me.

I tsk at him. "Uncle Fester. Quit terrorizing the birds."

He says nothing, just plops his butt down and licks a paw.

THE CARDINALS WERE RIGHT: it's been a good day. A massive thunderstorm blew in out of nowhere, so it's kept all my sisters away from the greenhouse and apparently prevented Quinton Henry from coming. I think the air pressure might actually be helping, so I've made a note of the barometric pressure. I've spent hours on the love potion, extracting a fresh batch of Elysian Blossom essence and pulling all the ingredients together in a carefully controlled procedure. So far, it's gone absolutely perfectly. So perfectly that I think this is going to be the batch. *The* batch. Love potion number 69. I can't help but snicker.

The only step left is to add in the Elysian Blossom essence, and my body is humming with anticipation. But before I get it out of the fridge, I need a moment to reflect and appreciate how far I've come. This has been such a long road, one I've been on practically since I was born. To be here, on the precipice of succeeding at a goal my family never thought I'd make...it's freaking awesome.

I turn the dance music up and shimmy down the aisle as the rain lashes the surrounding glass, two-stepping and twirling without a care in the world. Life is good. I lean down to kiss a succulent, then skip a few plants down and give an air hug to Elmer, the giant aloe plant that's older than me. I'm contemplating a cartwheel when there's a booming knock on the glass door.

I jump, my hand flying to my heart. Who in the world...? It can't possibly be Quinton. No one would come out in this weather.

The music cuts out and the booming knock comes again. As I turn to see who it is, the door flies open as a thunderclap echoes across the sky.

And there, in my doorway as lightning streaks through the clouds behind him, is a very wet, incredibly gorgeous, highly pissed-off man.

QUINTON

I HONESTLY DON'T intend for the door to go flying open when I bang on it, but I've had a shit day, so it's completely on brand at this point. I'm soaked, and I've just about had it. I can be forgiven for snarling at the woman who's standing halfway down a row of plants and gaping at me. And I can *definitely* be forgiven for stepping inside the blessedly dry building without waiting for an invitation.

"You can't—" she says behind me as I shut the door.

My toes squish inside my loafers as I turn. "Are you Clementine Rowan?"

She blinks at me, and as I drip, I take a moment to gather my wits.

Except they're gone. Because I meet her moss-green eyes right as another clap of thunder rattles the greenhouse, and it might as well be rattling my very soul.

The woman seems to have gotten over her shock. "You," she sneers.

Yep. This is definitely Clementine Rowan. I straighten and crack my neck, trying to ignore the way my blood heats at the sight of her.

"You're him," she says, her dark hair beginning to collapse out of its messy bun. "Quinton Henry."

And you're mine. I blink the thought away and doff an imaginary cap at her, managing to flick droplets of water on my face in the process. "In the flesh."

She crosses her arms, and the movement causes a pencil to fall out of her bun. Her hair unwinds, curling in a frizzy mess of waves around her face and down her back. "How did you find me?"

I step farther in and look around, both to break eye contact and to find something to dry my face and hands with. Spotting a gingham tea towel on the table that seems to be a makeshift laboratory of some sort, I make my way to it and pluck it up.

"Um, *excuse you*," Clementine says as I put it to my face without a second thought.

Then I smell it. It's so much more intense than what I've been exposed to all these years. Has she extracted its essence? I press the towel to my nose and inhale deeply, noting the hint of citrus and...hmm. I need more time. "Is this it? Elysian Blossom?" I glance at her, forcing myself to ignore how stunning she is with that angry red flush on her face, and bury my nose in the fabric for another whiff.

She's in front of me in seconds, yanking the towel away and crumpling it between her hands. "It's none of your business! Where do you get off waltzing in here and making yourself at home? I thought they taught manners to Canadians."

I wave at the weather outside, the day's events spiking my irritation back into full bloom. "Seriously? Listen, *Miss Rowan*, between nearly missing my flights—plural—then my rental car confirmation being unaccountably missing from the company's system, and *then* being unable to find a car service of any sort and having to hitch a ride to the hotel with a guy who I swear took a bath in garlic and onions, and then walking here *in this weather*, I have had a hell of a day. And if you'd just answered your phone like a normal person, I wouldn't be here!"

She stomps. Literally stomps. It's infuriatingly adorable, and the urge to gather her to me and kiss her is almost insurmountable. "I don't answer my phone when I'm working!" she retorts, then pushes her glasses up.

I nearly wince at the way her eye contact shoots straight to my dick, but I'm here to get a job done. So I take a deep breath and exhale. "Can we start over, please?" I ask.

It startles her. "What?"

I throw on my most devastatingly sexy smile. "Hello. I'm Quinton Henry. Nice to meet you." I step nearer to her and hold my still-damp hand out, half hoping she doesn't take it and more than half dying to touch her in any way possible.

Warily, she closes the distance and shakes my hand as another lightning bolt crackles above us. My body fizzes with the electric charge, nearly freezing me in place for a millisecond, and my brain decides to use that time to pack up all logic and hop the nearest train out of the station.

Clementine yanks her hand out of mine and shakes it, pressing it against her apron and scowling. "What are you up to?"

The movement is enough for me to notice the burn mark on her arm, and I want to rage and demand who hurt her. *What the hell is wrong with me?* I need to focus. "Me? I'm just trying to have a normal business meeting. *You're* the one working in a glass house in a thunderstorm and brewing god knows what in here. I should ask you what *you're* up to." I can taste the electricity on my tongue, and if anything, it increases my desire for her. I clench my jaw.

She rolls her eyes. "Your trip here was unnecessary. I told you no. My answer is still no." Then she turns, dismissing me, and walks to the refrigerator. Her dark hair falls all the way to an absolutely edible ass, and I bite back a moan as she opens the fridge and bends to retrieve something. I step closer to her, literally unable to stop myself. It's as though I'm watching myself from above, screaming to stop whatever the hell it is I think I'm doing, and yet still my body walks.

Clementine straightens, a vial of clear liquid in her hand, and strides to the workbench. I smell it immediately. *Elysian Blossom.* My hunch has to be right: that vial must hold the flower's essence. But doesn't it bloom only once every hundred years? It's a serious logistical issue my manufacturing team was going to have to hurdle, but one step at a time. First up was to get the seeds.

But if she's figured out how to extract its essence? Holy *shit*. I have to have her.

No, Quinton, what the fuck? I have to win her over—I'm here for her flower seeds, not her damn body.

Both.

Exasperated and feeling slightly feverish, I shake my head and follow her to the bench as she continues to ignore me. She sets the vial down and winds her hair into a bun, securing it with another pencil. She consults the notepad beside her, and I pull out my phone. If I can just get close enough...

She pivots to glare at me, but she's flushed. She feels it, too. "Why are you still here?" she demands.

Unable to step away from her, I shove my cell back in my pocket and clear my throat. "I'm sure we can come to an arrangement, Clementine."

She raises an eyebrow. "I liked it better when I was Miss Rowan."

I will call her anything she will let me. I draw closer and lower my voice, hoping she'll lean closer. Hoping my sanity can hang on. "Miss Rowan, then. Is that Elysian Blossom essence?"

She flushes even deeper and blinks rapidly behind her glasses. "Y-yes."

I'm close enough now that I'm surrounded by scents, and I can't tell which are from Clementine herself and which are coming from the various tubes on the workbench in front of us. I try to pick through them, but instead of extracting specifics, the logic side of my brain seems to grow tall like a wave, then squish and crumple on top of the emotional side. I feel drunk, fizzy. I can't feel my face. The edges of my vision seem to blur, and it's hard to focus on anything but the pulse fluttering in Clementine's neck. Clementine, in fact, is the only thing that is crystal clear. Judging by the way her chest is heaving, I'm betting she's just as affected as I am.

"Do you feel that, Miss Rowan?" I murmur. I reach out to touch her waist, and I know I shouldn't. It's not appropriate. I couldn't stop if a sword was about to chop my hand off.

She hisses at the contact, closing her eyes and swallowing hard. "Yes," she rasps.

My head is a mess. I scramble for scents, anything to focus on, and there, blinking in the recesses of my mind, are words. Identifications. Vanilla, musk, cinnamon, citrus, moss, a meadow drenched in sunshine, a willow tree, Clementine writhing beneath me, begging me to touch her as cardinals perch above us. Nothing makes sense. I just need to sort this out...I need...*fuck*.

"Quinton?"

I blink and shake my head again, trying to pull back to reality, to the rain lashing against the glass not five feet from me, the thunder rolling above us. "Clementine."

She steps away, putting too much distance between us, and immediately I want to feel her again. "I think..."

I'm pulled to her like a damn magnet. "Please just finish

what you were doing," I bite out, fighting for any sense of normalcy. "Then maybe…"

"Maybe whatever this is—"

"Will stop," I finish, meeting her eyes. God*damn* her eyes. Every green ever created is in there, flecks of lime set against the facets of gemstone emerald and sage and mossy olive. "*Please*," I urge, then fall helplessly again into the wonder that is Clementine Rowan.

CLEMENTINE

I CAN'T FEEL my legs. My body buzzes, hyper-aware of the man beside me. This can't be happening.

It's happening, the voice inside me whispers.

"Please," Quinton says again, then licks his full lips.

His beard looks so soft. So shiny. The curls seem to curve over themselves.

"*Clem.*"

I jerk my hand back, unaware it'd come within an inch of cupping his chin. "Right. Focus. I can focus."

Gritting my teeth, I grab the glass container in my right hand, swirling the liquid already in there and holding it up to the light. It's still good, clear, perfect. As though the last few minutes haven't even happened. I feel his eyes on my burn, his gaze not hateful but curious. Taking a breath, I grip the Elysian Blossom essence in my left hand.

Please let this work.

I'm dimly aware of how close Quinton has gotten, and I watch as his hand closes around my own, helping to pour the essence in.

It doesn't cloud.

Instead, streaks of pink and orange begin to appear in the jar as soon as the essence touches the liquid, funneling into a tornado that turns purple, then flattens out. The color is gone almost as quickly as it appears, leaving only a clear liquid in its wake. Outside, the wind howls as another round of thunder cracks through the sky.

"What just happened?" Quinton asks, his voice sounding as dazed as I am. Both his hands grip my waist now, and I press against him, utterly unable to make myself stop.

Peering at the liquid, I whisper, "Did it work?"

Quinton lowers his head with me, staring at the potion as though it has the answer to everything and breathing in the scent. It's floral, musky, citrusy, a fire in the hearth and a salty ocean all at once, and it's intoxicating. Excitement thrums through me. "I've done it. I've done it!" I yell over the thunder, drunk with victory and accomplishment.

"It's so similar to ours," he murmurs, "yet so different."

I don't know what he's talking about, but it doesn't matter. Because I've turned to him and am staring into his dark eyes, his pupils blown with need, and I can't stop myself from pulling his mouth to mine. I need him, more than I have ever needed anyone, and even though there's a very small, rational part of me screaming that none of this makes sense and to stop everything, the rest of me will not tolerate anything other than getting this man's mouth on mine.

The second our lips touch, the electricity I'd felt earlier pings around my body, practically boiling my blood as I surge up, wrapping my arms around him. The groan that comes out of both of us is pure sex as I press against his deliciously hard body. His beard is just as soft as I'd thought, and it doesn't scratch my skin at all. I shove his soaked jacket off his shoulders and he pulls my apron up and off, knocking my glasses against my forehead and grinning almost bashfully as he does it. Somewhere in the recesses of my mind, I notice the sweet look and wonder if that's the real Quinton—shy, bashful—but it's gone before I can hold on to it, falling through my thoughts like sand through a sieve. I toss my glasses onto the bench.

"Fucking knew you were like this under that ridiculous apron," he mutters, sliding his hands under my shirt and seeming to map my body.

I hiss at the contact, unable to remember the last time anyone touched me like their very life might depend on it. I scramble for his skin, needing to know if he's just as stupidly hot underneath that scowl as I suspect he is, and yes, god almighty *yes* he is, his torso thick but taut, his abdomen flexing beneath my touch.

More. I need more. Our mouths clash against each other, teeth knocking before he steadies my head with his hand and slants his lips across mine. The surge of his tongue into my mouth, needy and insistent, hints at what's to come. I undo his pants and shove a hand against the cotton of his briefs, a rush of excitement surging through me at the hardness I find there. His kisses are drugging, long, deep pulls that urge me to give him everything, all of it, forever and ever, amen.

"Clementine," he says, nipping at my chin, then neck. "What is happening?"

"Shut up," I murmur. "Keep going."

Then he's pushing a hand into my leggings and between my legs, and I moan against his mouth as one finger slides through my folds, then another. I sag against him, suddenly boneless, and he moves us so I'm against the workbench, his hand expertly working me as I clutch at his soggy button-down.

He lifts my shirt with his free hand and his mouth is hot and wet on the hollow of my throat as he bends, my hands clutching at air, then scrambling for purchase on the bench as he yanks my bra down and takes a nipple into his mouth, his fingers still working me. I gasp, muttering incoherently as he pulls off my breast and kneels, pulling my leggings down as he goes.

Then his mouth is on me, his tongue on my clit, his fingers thrusting inside of me, his other hand banded around my waist to keep me upright. The wind howls, and it sounds like hail is pelting the glass, and all I can do is moan and chant *yes, yes, yes* as Quinton's tongue works its magic.

It feels like my entire body is going to come. Pleasure threads through me, a ribbon coursing through every limb before circling back to my core, knotting into a bow and pulling tighter, tighter. The light flickers as thunder rumbles, and I look down. Quinton is pressed against me, his mouth on my pussy, and as I stare, he flicks his eyes up, meeting mine, and it's the hottest thing I have ever experienced in my life.

His fingers find that perfect spot inside of me and press. Lightning streaks across the sky as my legs tense and I throw my head back, giving myself over to the pleasure as it crests. Quinton's tongue and mouth and fingers keep going, and my whole body stiffens, then seems to explode as I come. Thunder rattles the windows as I scream, then sob as he pulls the orgasm out of me, the bliss greater than anything I've known.

Sucking in a breath, I meet Quinton's eyes once more, and another flash of lightning streaks across the sky as the power goes out.

For a moment, everything is utterly dark, the only sound the rain now falling soft as a kitten outside.

It's enough time for sanity to hit, and I scramble away from him as I pull up my leggings. What have I done? "Out," I manage to say between deep gulps of air. "Get out."

Another flash of lightning illuminates Quinton, standing

but bent over with his hands on his knees, staring at me in wonder, confusion, and outright lust.

I'm positive the same look is on my face.

"Out," I repeat.

Another flicker, another glance. Now he's right in front of me, his shirt half-unbuttoned, his tie—he had a tie?—askew, his skin luminous.

He smells so good.

I shake it off. No. No, none of this should have happened.

He wraps an arm around me and tips my chin up to take my mouth with his. His kiss is commanding, sensual, heady. The darkness whispers to me, promising that there's more here than meets the eye, if only I'm willing to look.

I pull away.

"You need to go," I say.

"We're not finished," he says, threading his hand through the hair at the nape of my neck. "I need—"

"To go. Quinton, you need to go." I step away from him, grasping for any shred of clarity I have left. As my heart rate slows, I notice how quiet it is outside. It's stopped raining.

In the dark, Quinton blows out a breath and swears. "What just happened?"

"Nothing," I insist. "Whatever this was, it doesn't matter, because it can't happen again."

Lightning appears in the sky again, silent, and my eyes meet Quinton's.

There's more, the voice insists.

In the glow of the lightning, Quinton opens his mouth, then closes it. It's clear he's struggling to understand, but I'm in no mood to enlighten him. I'm still not certain myself.

"Clementine," he says, his voice both uncertain and urging.

Silently, I grab my phone and flip on the flashlight, angling it toward the ground where Quinton's jacket lay. I keep my gaze locked there, even as I see him out of the corner of my eye running a hand over his face and studying me. After a beat, he picks up the jacket and turns to me. "Tomorrow, then."

When I say nothing, he shakes his head and leaves, trailing his unmistakable scent of a pine tree in winter with him. A scent that I've yearned for my whole life, but didn't know it until now.

QUINTON

I'D LIKE A word with the manufacturer of these hotel blinds, because they are doing an utterly shit job at their one function. The morning sun is not only slanting into the room, but the rays are beaming right into my eyeballs, and I can guarantee that I am, by far, the least-rested man in this fucking building.

Groaning, I feel for my cell and turn off the sound app that I'd finally downloaded in a last-ditch effort to get some modicum of sleep last night. The silence that follows reminds me of the utter lack of noise that followed last night's…experience.

I don't understand what happened. All I know is that I took one look at Clementine, and I needed her, with every cell of my body. Grand-mère liked to tell the story of how her and Papá fell in love at first sight, and I never believed it. But after last night?

I don't know. Maybe I do.

Shit got even more weird once we touched. It was like I was electrocuted by *her*, even though that's not possible, but after that, I needed to be near her, no matter what. I had to have her. And that was *before* that pink and orange tornado shit happened with the Elysian Blossom essence. Before I had my mouth on her and my fingers in her. Tasting her. Her coming on my tongue.

Uggggghhhh. I rub my hands over my face and get out of bed, ignoring the persistent hard-on I've had since I was on my knees in front of Clementine Rowan. I'm not getting any more sleep. And if I'm not, then neither is she.

I ignore the text that comes in from my dad asking how things are going and get ready. My suit is miraculously not ruined after last night, but my shoes are an entirely different story. Unfortunately, they're all I brought, so I squelch my feet into them and head to the lobby for some terrible hotel coffee and questionable pastry. There's a bowl of fruit, and I can't help the grin on my face as I grab two clementines for the road.

After a ten-minute walk that is far more pleasant than last night, I'm back at the Rowan house. I stand on the sidewalk in front of it for a good two minutes, taking in the heft of it, the way it seems to both loom and welcome, to shoo and embrace. *A bit like Miss Rowan.*

"Well, are you coming in or not?"

I jolt back to awareness and lay my eyes on a woman leaning in the doorway, arms crossed and wearing a knowing smile. I struggle to pull her into focus as I make my way up the short walkway; she's almost blurred at the edges. She's darker-skinned than Clementine and her eyes are amber-colored, but the family resemblance is clear in the way she holds herself and seems to look down on me, despite me being a good foot taller than her. Her hair is long and wavy like Clementine's, too, but where Clementine's is a rich brown, this woman's hair is so blonde it's nearly white. The whole effect of her is otherworldly, and she doesn't help matters by the way her eyes pierce into me in a way that feels a little intrusive.

All the same, I hold my hand out. "Quinton Henry."

She lifts a brow at the hand and pushes off the doorframe. "I know who you are. We all do, Quinton." She turns and saunters into the house, calling back as she goes. "Come on. I've made you tea."

I look around, unsure if it's for help or simply a witness to my impending doom, and follow.

The inside is a colorful clutter of organized mess, and I'm guessing that several people live here. I move through a narrow hallway, various rooms and stairways branching off with no discernible logic, and I'm in the kitchen within moments. The woman waits, standing at a small round table that holds only four chairs, and she smiles at my clear confusion. "Clementine is coming, Quinton. How was your trip from Coal's Lake? Not *too* terrible, I hope?"

I narrow my eyes, suspicious of the question. "It could have been better."

Her laugh is like little alarm bells going off in my head. "Oh, goodness, I'm so sorry. I sometimes think we get a little carried away. It wasn't a full moon, so we thought...well, never mind." She waves her hand, then gestures for me to sit. "Tea?"

The plastic of the seat cushion groans as I take a seat. Carried away? By what? And what's a full moon got to do with my traveling? "I didn't catch your name. Where did you say Clementine was?"

She smiles wide, a huntress eyeing her prey. "I'm Willow. One of Clem's sisters."

A puzzle piece clicks into place. *Trees.* They're named after trees. "Are there more of you?" I watch as she pours the tea from a pot that looks incredibly fragile.

"Seven of us total," Willow says.

I nod absently, leaning closer to get a better look at the teapot's toile pattern. "Those flowers—those are Elysian Blossom, right?"

She looks at me appreciatively as I take a sip. "Perhaps you *are* more than a pretty face, Mr. Henry."

I'm about to protest—I am definitely more than a pretty face—and then ask if maybe she's the one to talk to about the Elysian Blossom seeds, but the taste of the tea hits me. It's unlike anything I've ever tasted. "This is delicious."

Willow grins and throws her shoulders back. "It *is*, isn't it?"

I sip again, searching for the ingredients she's used. Perfume and tea can often use the same building blocks. Chrysanthemum, willow bark (no surprise there), apple… and more I can't quite pinpoint. I take another sip, rolling the liquid around on my tongue. "Tell me, what's in here?"

"What are you serving him?" Clementine's voice is sharp and no-nonsense as she enters the kitchen.

I swallow another huge gulp and stand, turning and hoping I can keep it together this time. *Come on, Q. You can do this, man.*

And, shit.

She's luminous in the morning light, dressed in black jeans and a black t-shirt that has Flower Child spelled on it in a graphic flower font. Her dark hair, glossy and thick, hangs down her back and front like a Disney princess's, and her gorgeous green eyes are soft as they look at me from behind her wire-rimmed glasses. She bites back a smile. "Good morning, Quinton," the love of my life says.

Am I making moon eyes at her? Probably. "Good morning, Clementine," I manage to respond. "You look wondrous."

Clementine flushes, her olive skin deepening prettily as she blinks. "Thank you."

The wooden chair I'm holding onto for dear life creaks in protest, and behind me, Willow snickers and murmurs, "Never seen it do this before."

Clementine seems to gather herself, and her eyes flash in accusation at her sister. "You *didn't*."

I can't look away from Clementine, but it sounds like Willow shrugs as she says, "Of course I did. Couldn't pass up the opportunity."

Wait. My fingers are prickling, like they've been asleep and the blood is just now flowing back into them. "Did you put something into that tea?" I ask, finally able to look at Willow now that Clementine has moved to stand next to her at the sink.

It's nice to see that Clementine isn't mad at me this morning, but I *almost* feel sorry for Willow, because Clementine is seething as she says, "You had no right to do that! He's messed up enough as it is—"

"Hey!" I protest. "I'm right here. And there's nothing wrong with me. My fingers are tingling, but that's it." I peer at the remnants of the tea in my cup. "What'd you use to make it do that?"

"Not. A. Word," Clementine says to her sister.

Willow snaps her mouth shut and makes a *what are you gonna do?* gesture.

"Out. Get out!" Clementine says, and Willow laughs.

"Fine, I'm leaving," she says. "Aspen and Mom need my help at the store anyway." She breezes out of the room, brushing by me as she does. "I like you," she whispers. "Good luck."

Both charmed and slightly unnerved by those words, I turn my attention wholly to Clementine. "We need to talk, but can I kiss you first?"

She blinks. "You honestly still feel this?"

I draw near, not able to be in the same room as her and

remain so far away. "Nothing has changed since last night, Clementine. From the moment I saw you…" I shake my head, still unsure how to describe it. "I need you," I finally say, pulling her hands into mine. My body hums with a sense of rightness the second I touch her.

Her irises dilate and her lips part as she heaves a breath. "What you're feeling…it's not real, Quinton," she croaks. "Between last night and just now…none of it's real."

I pull her to me, wrapping my arms around her waist and marveling at how perfectly we fit together. "Of course it is," I murmur, leaning down to her upturned lips.

She stills, and as I take her mouth with mine, a sense of deep contentment settles inside my chest. *I'm home.* I'm precisely where I've always been meant to be. I feel Clementine's arms wrap around my neck, and I know, I *know*, she feels it, too. She opens, letting me in, and the kiss is nothing like last night's urgency. This is soft, tender. Proof of love. Inside the kiss I see the Clementine I'm meant to know, the one where she's my love until we're old and wrinkled. I see our children playing under a willow tree and hear their giggles in Clementine's tiny sigh as I cup her face with my hands.

"Quinton," she breathes, and as I stare at those moss-colored eyes, all I can know is I love her. It doesn't make sense, but it doesn't have to. We barely know each other, but we know enough.

"Can we talk?" It's all I can think to say. Distantly, in the recesses of my mind, I know that I still need to sort out the deal for my family. That my mom and dad and grand-mère are counting on me. But right now, none of that matters. All that matters is the woman in front of me.

Then her eyes shutter. "There's nothing to talk about." She takes a firm step back, out of my reach, and I follow. "Quinton. Stop."

I stop moving. "But you—just now—you feel it, too," I plead. "Right? I know you do. I saw…" I let the words fall away. Because how do I tell her I saw our children—*plural*—under a tree when we kissed?

Her eyes widen, then narrow. "You saw what?"

I shake my head, holding on to the final shreds of logic. I won't admit what I saw. It was fantasy.

It wasn't.

I look around for the voice that just whispered those words. "Did you…? Never mind."

Clementine looks at me warily, then starts to back out of the kitchen. "Look, Quinton. My sisters like to play jokes, and that's all this is. One big joke. You shouldn't have come here. We're not selling you the seeds. Go home to Coal's Lake."

"What's the joke? The tea? It's fine. I'm fine," I insist, taking a tentative step towards her. I can't let her go. I don't know what she's talking about, but it doesn't matter.

"What we—I mean what *you're*—feeling. It's not real," she repeats.

"You were about to say 'we,' weren't you? It's not just me."

"Leave, Quinton. You don't belong here." She turns and runs out.

"Clementine, wait!" I call, but all I hear is a door shutting.

CLEMENTINE

M Y PHONE PINGS with a message right as I get into my car.

MAGNOLIA

> Don't forget you're speaking to my class! Be here in 15 minutes.

Did she *really* just send me a reminder with only fifteen minutes to get to the school and have an entire class presentation ready?

She did. She most definitely did.

And I could not be more grateful, because I was two seconds away from running back into the house, jumping on Quinton, and demanding he take me upstairs and bang the shit out of me. Which is a problem, because like I told him, none of this is real.

It's not.

I send Magnolia a thumbs up and start the drive to the school, happy I'd managed to put on deodorant and everything else required to leave the house and look like a functioning adult before walking into the kitchen this morning.

Sure, I'm in jeans that haven't been washed in a month and I had to do a sniff test on the shirt I grabbed off the floor and put on, but this is high school. The kids either don't care what they or anyone else looks like—and are therefore my people—or they care too much, and are therefore the people who gave me crap when I was there all of eight years ago. Hopefully the ratio has tilted in my favor over time.

I can't stop thinking about him. His eyes, so dark brown I could barely see the irises, had felt like a physical touch as they raked over me in the kitchen. I could practically feel his lips on mine again, feel the way they streaked a path, hot and fast, down to my very center and made me come harder than I'd ever come before in my life.

The tug I feel for him, the near-cellular insistence of my body that there's more to this than I realize, isn't real. It can't be. The immediate connection was caused by the love potion.

Then why haven't you told your family you made it?

I ignore that. Because just now, in the kitchen? That was because I put the potion on, like a perfume. I wanted to see if it worked. And obviously, it did.

See? Logic. Pure and simple.

Bullshit.

I FACE the camera on the locked school door and wait for Mrs. Hayes in the administration office to buzz me in. Yanking open the door, I wave at her as I walk past and point at my wrist to indicate I'm almost late, which is true, but which also helps me avoid a painful ten-minute chat with her while I sign the visitor's sheet.

I've never been in Magnolia's classroom, because she wasn't teaching at this school when I was here. She was teaching about thirty minutes away in Talladega, biding her time until old Mr. Carter finally decided to retire. The crotchety old goat was seventy-five when he finally put down his lab goggles, and if I hadn't despised the way he constantly pushed me in the classroom, insisting I could do better, I might have admired his longevity. Even now, I go out of my way to avoid him when I see his car in the parking lot of the grocery store or coffee shop.

The smell is the same, a bit of body odor mixed with vague scents of confusion and chemicals. Magnolia spots me through the window, smiles and gestures me in. "Class, this is my sister, Miss Clementine Rowan."

I lift my hand weakly and smile, straightening my spine and reminding myself that I am, in fact, a grown woman and need to act like it with these little twerps. Especially the one in the front, sneering at me like I'm some kind of slime she's unexpectedly found on her shoe.

There are times when I wish I really were the witch my classmates teased me about being.

I'm not one. But I'm not *not* one, either, so take that for what you want.

"Clementine?" Magnolia prompts.

Right. I lurch into it. "Hey. So, who likes flowers? I bet you do," I say to the girl who's still sneering at me. "Anyone want to take a guess at how many types are used for medicinal purposes?"

A kid raises his hand in the back. "Isn't aspirin made from flowers?"

I smile. "It's not."

"It's from willow bark, dumbass," another guy snarks.

"Also not precisely true," I lobby back, happy to shut him down. "There's a connection to the willow tree, though—the white willow tree and leaves have salicin in it, which can be converted to salicylic acid in the body. Egyptians used it, and so did the Roman physician Celsius and even Hippocrates. Things kicked into gear in 1763 in England to uncover exactly what was in the tree bark that was working, and that's how they uncovered salicin. By the early 1800s they could convert it to salicylic acid, and once they combined that knowledge with additional techniques in the lab, they were off and running."

The next twenty minutes are easy, with me asking the students various questions and bringing it back to how plants are at the root—ha, pun intended—of so much of modern medicine. "So what is it that you do, exactly?" the girl in the front asks.

I can't help the broad smile I give her. "I grow various flowers, shrubs and trees around our family property to be used in the teas we sell at the apothecary, and I'm working on some research of my own." I can't wait to finally tell my family what I've managed to do. I just want to recreate it one more time.

She sniffs. "Sounds boring."

I'm about to retort when movement out of the classroom door's window catches my attention. *No. Way.*

Magnolia stands, also seeing the tall drink of water that is Quinton Henry, and moves around her desk. "Thanks again for coming, Clementine." She holds her hands out, indicating I need to leave, but I'm frozen to the spot. "*Clem,*" she hisses. "*Move it.*"

I lurch forward, possibly because Magnolia gives me a push, and am out the door before I realize what's happening.

Quinton's face is almost predatory as he takes me in. "Clementine," he says, his voice low and velvety. "Just who I was looking for."

I begin to walk past him, unwilling and flat-out unable to

return the look, when he grabs my wrist. A zing of electricity shimmers through me again, far too similar to the one from last night to be a coincidence. And this time, there's no thunderstorm to blame.

"We aren't doing this here," I say, having no idea what I even mean by 'this' but knowing that my old high school is *not* the setting for whatever it is.

He whips in front of me, halting my progress so quickly that I bang right into him, and immediately his wintry pine scent fills my senses.

Mine.

The thought whips through me so thoroughly that I lose my breath, bouncing back from him and nearly tripping over my feet as I go. Quinton grabs for me, his broad hands encircling my upper arms to steady me, and as I look up, I see literal hearts twirling above his head. Pink and white and red, glittery and bright, twinkling at me like some kind of scene right out of a cartoon. I blink, but they're still there, and Quinton is still holding me, still steadying me as I try to understand what in the actual hell is happening. Again.

Then I realize: it's Valentine's Day. And the hearts that are above his head are in fact all over the place: hanging from the ceiling, stapled to the announcement board to my right, decorating the classroom doors up and down the hall. A relieved laugh escapes me, and it turns into something uncomfortably close to a hysterical giggle within seconds.

"Clementine? Are you okay?"

"Are you *kidding*?" I laugh. "Am I okay? No, no I'm not," I say. "I'm not remotely close to okay. Are you?"

He laughs. "Not at all."

"Exactly." I shake him off and speed-walking to the exit.

He's hot on my tail. "We have to talk about what's happening," he says. He keeps talking, saying everything that's already run through my head overnight and this morning, and all I can do is keep walking.

Once we're outside, I make a beeline for my car, knowing he's going to get in without an invitation and knowing with a bone-deep certainty that I'm going to let him. It's the potion. It has to be the potion.

It's the potion's fault that I aim the car for the hotel. It's the potion's fault that when we get there, I let him take my hand and lead me inside. And it's the potion's fault for the way I tumble into him as we step inside the room.

QUINTON

MY HANDS ARE shaking as I haul her to me and crush my lips to hers. I lose my breath, growing dizzy as our mouths fuse to each other, and the stars I see may very well be from lack of oxygen. I don't care.

After a moment, Clementine wrenches away, both of us gasping for air and staring at each other. "Are we doing this?" she asks, her eyes a deep shining emerald. "And to be clear, I don't know what this is. Did I say that already? Oh, god." She steps back, looking terrified.

I smile and hold my palm out for hers. She takes it, and another tingle passes into me from the touch. I squeeze her hand. "That right there," I say, looking down at our joined hands, "whatever that is? *That* is why we're doing this. I don't know what it is, either, Clementine. But I know this: you are, without a doubt, the sexiest, smartest, most infuriatingly hard-headed, stubborn woman I have ever met, and I absolutely need you."

"Do you have a condom?" she blurts.

"Always."

"Prove it."

"Always the scientist, eh?" I smile and walk to the bathroom to retrieve the handful in my dopp kit—years of living with Axl in Coal's Lake taught me to never leave home without them—and brandish them as I return. Her eyes follow me as I lay them on the bedside table and turn back to her. "I want you to know how hard it is not to tackle you right now."

She heaves a sigh and studies me. Then she cracks a smile, and I swear I hear lightning crackle across the sky. "Good enough for me," she says, then yanks out the pencil holding her hair up, and lunges.

I catch her with a *oh thank fuck* exhale, and in seconds she's peeling my suit jacket off and yanking my tie loose, then making quick work of my shirt.

"Why the hell did you wear a tie?" she mutters, her small, warm hands exploring my chest.

"Because they make me—" I hiss in a breath as she runs her thumbs over my nipples—"feel like I know what I'm doing."

She chuckles. "How's that going for you?"

"Fucking awesome," I answer, shoving her biker jacket down, pulling her shirt over her head, then snapping her bra off. "Jesus," I whisper as I finally get a good look at her in the light. "Clementine…"

She tips her chin high, and the movement cracks something deep inside my chest. The burn on her arm goes all the way up to her shoulder, splattering onto the top part of a pert breast. "I was six."

I shake my head. "You misunderstand. You're perfect, Clementine."

She blushes, her cheeks deepening in the late morning light and making her even more gorgeous. Wordlessly, I bend to take a mouth-watering nipple in my mouth, listening for her reaction and adjusting as I go. This woman will get whatever she needs and wants from me, and then some. She moans as I band an arm around her waist, and it seems to flip the switch.

Need screams to the surface, raw and unfettered, shredding all pretense of subtlety and patience. Our hands are on each other's pants, yanking them down and off along with underwear, shoes and socks, until we're completely naked, then I'm walking backwards and we're falling into the bed, our mouths all over each other, teeth and tongues and panting, and I'm beside her, trailing my hand down between her legs to feel her warmth. She spreads her legs, and I dip my fingers between her folds.

She closes her eyes, luxuriating in the feel as my thumb finds and circles that perfect bundle of nerves. I kiss her temple, her forehead, her sloped nose, her cupid's bow lips. She's a wood nymph come to life, and as she pushes her fingers against my hair, humming at the pleasure I'm giving her, I wonder at how I've gone this long without her. Because it's obvious, so fucking obvious, that she was meant for me. It's in the way we're breathing in synch. It's in the way I'm already so tuned into her, how I knew exactly where to find her this morning, how the rest of the world seems to fall away when her eyes open and settle on mine.

I push one finger into her, the both of us moaning at the movement, then I pull it out and add another. "Tell me what you like," I whisper, crooking my fingers inside her, then doing it all over again. Her muscles tense around my efforts. She's close.

"This," she mews. "How do you—*fuck*," she breathes.

"There you go," I say. "Come for me, Sprite."

She stills, her entire body stiffening for a moment, then she yells my name as she comes apart, her chest blooming with a deep blush that looks exactly like the blooms of the Elysian Blossom. Because of course it does. I kiss her as she rides the orgasm out on my hand, and before I realize what she's doing, she's flipped me onto my back and is straddling me, her wet heat sliding across my bare cock.

"Fuck, Clementine." It's almost a prayer.

She rises up and leans for a condom, her dark hair curtaining over her body as she moves. Keeping the foil between two fingers, she shifts, moving between my legs and seeming to hum in delight at what she finds.

"Damn, Q," she says naughtily, her emerald eyes gleaming as she looks up at me. I clench my fists, nearly coming at the very sight of her poised above my cock and licking her lips. "You're working with some serious stuff here." Still kneeling, she pulls her hair over to the side and twists it, then hands the condom to me. "You're gonna want to hold this."

"Holy fucking *shit*, Clementine."

She laughs, a deep, satisfied sound that I did not expect to come out of her. Her lips twitch, then she says, "Oh, sweetheart, you're mine. Love potion or not. Real or not. This dick is mine."

I don't know what she's talking about, but I don't give a fucking god damn because she's right, I'm hers, always. "Yours," I say, then groan as she licks the tip.

"Watch," she commands, wrapping one hand around the base of my shaft and the other around my balls, and I swear to god, I have never in my life been more turned on than I am right now. So I do. I watch her suck my cock like a fucking champion, and it takes all of sixty seconds before I'm warning her that I'm about to come.

She increases her work, humming and pumping, but I'm not having it. I scoot out from beneath her, heaving, damn near glaring at her for almost making me lose it.

"Woman," I growl.

She raises her eyebrows saucily and shrugs. "I told you. It's mine."

And it's here, in the middle of a hotel bed in Sacred River, with Clementine on her knees and declaring my cock is hers with absolutely no apology, that I officially fall in love with her.

CLEMENTINE

QUINTON LAUGHS AND shakes his head. He's on his back, propped up on his elbows and looking up at me, his golden brown skin absolutely flawless against the white sheets, his chest flecked with a smattering of black curls.

He is delicious.

And I can't stop this anymore. Can't fight the constant pull to be near him, to touch him, to be touched by him. I know it's the love potion—how else does something like this happen?—but I have to give in. Letting go, watching his face, seeing how he looks at me as though I am a goddess sent from above for him and him alone as I roll the condom on, it feels like sinking into a perfectly warm bath. Everything is relaxed inside me, content.

As I lower myself onto him, we both go quiet. Quinton's fingers dig into my hips as we breathe, his dark eyes unmoving from mine. I read his every feeling in there, and I know they mirror my own. I raise again, lowering another bit, then do it again and again until I'm so full of him it's almost too much.

"Quinton," I breathe, "you feel so good."

"That's not the right word." He skims his hands down my thighs and back up, curving my ass and up to my back. "Incredible is better."

I nod and start to move. He groans as I manage, "Delicious," the word from my earlier thought rising to the surface.

"Fuck, you're so tight," he says.

I am. The partners I've had have been few and far between, and none of them were Quinton's size. All I can do is throw my head back in agreement as I find my rhythm, swirling and moving up and down. When he cups my breasts, I place my hands over his, showing him how I want to be touched. He's a quick study, and as his thumbs coast over my nipples, I squeeze my inner walls.

He grunts, using his hips to thrust deeper into me. I hitch a breath and fall forward, my hands on his chest as my hair falls around us, blocking out the world. Our eyes meet again and we stop talking, nothing but the sound of our breath filling the air. When he reaches to cradle my chin, angling his torso up, I'm already bending down to meet him.

I swear I hear a rumble of thunder as we kiss, or maybe it's my heart cracking wide open. All I know is that this kiss feels different. Tender and loving, exploring, learning. His lips are soft, luscious and thick like the rest of him, but he yields to me without question, following my lead as I nip at his lower lip, then upper. I plunder his mouth, wondering all over again at the softness of his beard, how it doesn't hurt the sensitive skin around my mouth at all.

When he whispers, "Let me on top," I go willingly, happy to cede control.

As he settles between my hips, he brushes my hair back, he scans my face as though he's memorizing me, learning me. I do the same, noting the freckles dotting his nose, the hint of baby crow's feet at the corners of his eyes, the way they crinkle in delight as he takes me in.

"Tell me your full name," he murmurs.

"Clementine Amelia *fuck*," I swallow the word as he thrusts into me, "Rowan." Oh god. He might tear me apart and I will die a happy woman. I pull my knees up, opening wider for him as he cages his arms around my head.

"Quinton Anthony Robert Henry the second," he pants, grabbing one of my legs and changing the angle.

I quirk a grin. "Nice to meet you."

"Figured you should know the name of your future kid," he grins back.

I don't hesitate. "The one playing under the willow tree?"

His eyes flare as he pushes again.

"Always wondered what his name was," I gasp.

He pauses, pulls my leg over his shoulder, and thrusts home again. I let out a growl to match his own, and then he says, "Anthony."

"What he goes by? Jesus *fuck* Quinton you feel so good," I say, my teeth clenched.

"Can't have you calling out our son's name when I fuck you, babe," he says, then pounds me.

My orgasm starts to crest and all I can do is hold on, panting and swearing and calling his name, my entire world condensed to the man surrounding me, consuming me, loving me. When it comes, the orgasm overrides all thought, all logic, washing through my body like an electric surge of power. There's no stopping the animalistic yell that comes out of me, or the way I clutch Quinton to me, needing every bit of his skin and mouth possible, needing him, always him.

Quinton holds me tight, his hips pumping as he chases his own pleasure, and he's there seconds behind me, shouting into my ear, both of us tightly bound to the other.

In the stillness that follows, all I can do is breathe, my

chest heaving into his as my heartbeat slows, dimly aware of the way my legs are pretzeled. I'm surrounded by his wintry pine scent, and my head fills with an image of a snow-bound forest, ice cracking the branches, the white snow twinkling from the sun's rays in the bluebird sky above. In the distance, a figure tracks through the landscape, his face tilted up to the sun. I know, without question, that it's Quinton, and that it's only the first of many images I'll see.

The realization is a tectonic shift, because I've never had it happen. Maybe there's more to my gift than I've known. Or maybe it's Quinton, or maybe the love potion…and that thought hurts more than it should.

Slowly, Quinton shifts and lets my leg down, and I sigh at the release it brings. His eyes narrow in concern. "Did I hurt you?"

I shake my head, a gentle smile on my face. "No. Never."

He grins and pushes hair away from my sweaty face with soft fingers. "This is crazy, right?"

"Not in my family," I say.

He raises an eyebrow. "I'm intrigued, but hold that thought." He rolls out of the bed and I watch as he strides to the bathroom to dispose of the condom.

I'm grateful for the daylight, because I get to see this man's incredible butt, bracketed by a muscular back and legs, and when he returns, I catalogue his thick, corded body, the darker bits of skin on his knees, the way his ridiculous cock sways a bit as he walks. Big Dick Energy for the win, ladies, and *I'm* the one who's winning.

"What's that smile for?" Quinton asks as he slides back into the bed and pulls the covers up to his waist.

I laugh. "Just enjoying the view," I say.

He goes onto his side and props his head in his hand. "Glad I could be of service."

"In so many ways," I snicker.

He bops my nose with his finger. "So naughty," he says fondly.

I twist my lips. "This is a very recent development."

"Yeah?"

"Like in the last twenty-four hours recent."

His laugh is warm and decadent, dark chocolate chip cookies right out of the oven, and I scoot closer to him on instinct. He reaches for me, pulling me to him and guiding a leg between his. "Talk to me, Sprite. Tell me everything."

I wrinkle my nose. "Not sure about this nickname, Q."

His eyes soften. "You're tiny."

"I'm five feet two inches—that is not tiny!" I protest.

He snorts. "Keep telling yourself that. Is wood nymph better?"

"Ew, no." I try to scoot away, but it only makes him gather me closer and shift us, my stomach to his side, our legs threaded together, my head on his chest, my fingers tracing his soft skin.

"How many kids are we having?" His question is a rumble in my ear.

"Three," I answer. "One boy—the only boy—and two girls."

He hums. "How are we both so calm about this?"

I flatten my palm against his chest and run it down to his side, his hip, his powerful thigh. "Because I made a love potion."

He stiffens, then pulls away to look down at me. "Say what?"

I sigh. May as well get this over with. I sit up and cross my legs, pulling the sheet to cover my lap. His eyes linger on my breasts before making their way back up to meet my gaze. "The night you showed up. The potion we put together?"

He nods. "The pink and orange makes purple tornado in the crazy-ass thunderstorm?"

"The very one. That was love potion number sixty-nine."

He snorts another laugh. "Sixty-nine? Come on." He waggles his eyebrows. "If that's what you wanted, you just had to say it." He makes to dive under the covers, but I stop him.

"It's true," I say, giggling and swatting at him. "I'd tried sixty-eight other times to get it right. It just *happened* to be sixty-nine when you showed up."

Still grinning, he says, "Okay, so...*love potion*? Tell me more."

"For generations, my family was known for this particular potion. It was said to quite literally be a love potion: the person would wear it around their crush or whatever, and boom, love." And as the words come out, I realize that's what this is. Swallowing, I continue. "But my great-grandmother died without teaching it to my grandmother or mother, and it was never written down. Everyone figured it was lost to history, but I'm a freaking botanist. I wanted to recreate it. I knew it was tied to the Elysian Blossom, because it only grows here, and family lore also said that it couldn't be made that often. So the first thing I had to do was figure out how to get it to bloom on demand. That took a year. Then it was a matter of sorting out the ingredients. My mom could remember what it smelled like, but literally nothing else."

Quinton chuckles. "Sounds familiar."

I peer at him. "What do you mean?"

"I mean the reason I've been blowing you up for the same damn flower: my family is counting on me to recreate the perfume that made us famous. And my dad—who is so talented that his nose is literally insured for millions—is blind to the Elysian Blossom scent. But I'm not."

I pick at a loose thread on the sheet and blow out a breath. "So we're both trying to use the flower to create a legendary scent for our families." I glance up and meet his steady gaze. "And I didn't get mine to work until you were beside me, literally helping pour the Elysian Blossom essence into the rest of the potion. Once that happened, we..." I shrug and look back down, pulling on the thread again.

When I can't handle the silence anymore, I look up to find him studying me. "Do you honestly think that's what this is? What *we* are?" he asks, gesturing between us. "The product of some kind of magical love potion?"

"It's the only explanation." *And the visions?* A fluke. That's all they are.

"No."

His voice is so deep, so insistent, that it startles me. "It's true, Quinton."

"No, Clementine." He shifts, sitting up to face me and pulling my hands into his. "I will freely admit that this is a little...different. Hell, we were talking about *kids* just a few minutes ago, at least one of whom we've both seen underneath a damn willow tree. So yeah, fine. This isn't one hundred percent logical. But it *is* one hundred percent real. I have to believe that."

"Why?"

He blinks.

I push. "*Why* do you have to believe it? Why can't you believe that all of this is precisely because of chemistry? Science has already proven that initial attraction has to do with our bodies' responses to other's pheromones. So why can't adding a potion—a scent designed to heighten that very response—be what this is?"

He's silent, and I can practically see the thoughts whirring in his head. Finally, he speaks. "Because I have never felt this way in my life. Because you drove me crazy when you were ignoring my calls and being a snarky little bellend by email, but I couldn't wait to see what you'd do or say next. Because you're clearly beloved by your family, even though the one sister I've met kind of scares me. Because you're driven. Because..." he looks away, as though to steel himself, and turns back. "Because my grandparents fell in love at first sight, and I did, too."

The world seems to blur and darken everywhere except the bubble that Quinton and I are in, and I catch my breath. Did he just say...

"Yes, I did."

"Oh my god." I scramble backwards and off the bed, panic searing through me. This is the absolute worst thing that could happen. "No. No. No. No, you can't be in love with me, Quinton—we barely know each other!"

"I do." His voice is calm, certain. "I love you."

I find my panties and step into them, whirling around to find he's been looking at my ass. "Stop looking at me!" I nearly screech. "This—you—*no!*" I repeat.

"Come on, Clementine," he says. "For one thing, your ass is fantastic. And if you take a moment to breathe, I bet we can talk this through."

I shove my arms through my bra straps and glare at him. "Did you just tell me to calm down?"

"Hell no." He holds his hands up. "We are well into the twenty-first century. I know better than that."

"That's one point in your favor," I mutter, glancing around for my pants.

"What's another one?"

I snatch my pants up and start putting them on, certain I misheard him. "What?"

"What's another point in my favor?" he says. "Something else you like about me."

The tiniest of smirks hits my face, and I turn away before he can see it.

"See? You like me."

Dammit. He saw it. "It doesn't matter," I say, putting my shirt on and grabbing for my socks.

"Of *course* it matters. I'm over here, butt-ass naked, telling you I love you, so you liking me definitely matters."

I giggle, my heart rate slowing back down after spiking in the face of his declaration. "Fine, I like you. But—"

"No buts. Unless we're still talking about my butt, or your butt, both of which are fantastic."

Another laugh escapes me. "Dammit, Quinton, be serious!"

He gets up and closes the distance between us, and my traitorous eyes scan his body as he approaches. Honestly, it's unfair. Men like him shouldn't be allowed to exist. "We can figure this out, Sprite."

"Stop calling me Sprite." I shove my feet into my shoes, trying mightily to keep my eyes to myself and failing miserably.

"I will helicopter my dick in your face if you don't look up here," he threatens, his tone full of amusement.

My cheeks heat as I meet his eyes, and my heart flops over at the adoration I see there. "I really want this to be real. I do. But how can we be sure?" I ask.

"We can't," he says matter-of-factly. "But does it matter?"

"Yes!" I say.

"Why?"

I close my eyes. "Can you please put some clothes on?"

He chuckles. "I'd rather you take yours back off, sweetheart.

I shrug my jacket on. "I need to go."

"We're not finished. You know that, right?" His voice is gentle.

"I know." But I need out of here. I need to clear my head, and breathe, and think, and I can't do that with Quinton around. He muddles me.

So I leave him there, naked, holding my heart in his hands.

CLEMENTINE

"YOU DID WHAT?" Mom stares at me, open-mouthed, while Willow and Magnolia remain carefully neutral.

"I made the love potion," I repeat, then push the bottle across the wooden counter towards her. "Smell it."

Mom raises an eyebrow. "I didn't know you kept working at it."

I squirm, self-conscious. "I didn't want it to just...disappear."

Mom's lips tip up as she glances to the front of the shop. It's almost five o'clock, so it's nearly time to close and the shop is empty. After leaving Quinton at the hotel, I'd headed straight to my greenhouse and spent hours working to successfully recreate the potion. And I'd done it, over and over again, as easy as you please. I had fifteen bottles already. As if I'd not spent five years working to get here, struggling and failing so much that I only started counting the combinations last year.

With every successful batch, I wanted to call Quinton, to turn and share my success with him. He was the only one I wanted to tell. Not Mom, not Magnolia, not any of my sisters. But I couldn't. Besides the whole love-potion-made-me-do-it aspect, there was also the part where he still wanted to buy the Elysian Blossom seeds for his company's use. Which, of course, I couldn't let happen. *You know what to do,* Mom had said.

So, yeah, I'd gotten the space from Quinton that I said I wanted. But I was no closer to clarity. In fact, the only thing I was certain of was that I couldn't get rid of an incessant ache in my chest, no matter what I did.

And that's why I was at the shop. I'd texted Mags to come after school, and Willow was already here. I'd rather have everyone around to show them the potion at once, but Aspen's out of town and Juniper and Jasmine are on a culinary road trip of some kind, and Hazel...well, Hazel's never here.

My heart beats faster as Mom slides the bottle close, then pulls the stopper out. Immediately the flowery scent fills the air, hints of hibiscus and lavender weaving in with eucalyptus and the particular scent of Elysian Blossom. Mom's bright blue eyes widen as she leans down to inhale. "It smells just like I remember," she says in wonder. "Clementine, you did it! I'm so proud of you!"

"Congratulations, little one," Willow says, her voice warm.

"That's amazing, Clementine," Magnolia gushes, pulling me into a fierce hug and seeming to conveniently forget all the shit she gave me just a few days ago.

I accept the hug and smile sadly. I'd wanted this for so long—had put every other dream and goal on hold so that I could finally make this one happen—and now that it's here, all I want to do is curl into a ball and cry.

"Tell us everything," Mom says, a huge smile on her face.

Then she ducks her head to get a better look at me. "Wait. What's wrong?"

Her concern, combined with the mere force of being the center of these three women's attention, is enough to make me burst into tears.

"Now you're *definitely* telling us everything," Mom says, nodding at the front door to lock it and guiding me to sit down on the stool set up at the old-timey soda fountain bar.

Willow and Magnolia flank me, and Mom bustles back around to make us some tea. In minutes, we're all sipping from Mom's "Make It All Better" blend, which I swear has some illegal ingredients in it, but Mom and Aspen swear it doesn't. Regardless, there's no denying the near-immediate calming effect the tea has on me, and I take a deep breath, hold it, and let it out.

"It's Quinton Henry, isn't it?" Mom says. "I told you—"

"Ooh, it *is* Quinton Henry," Willow says. "I thought for sure Magnolia and I scared him away with the weather."

"Don't bring me into this," Magnolia says.

"I wouldn't have known about him other than you telling me!" Willow protests.

"Girls, we've talked about this. Weather isn't something to be trifled with," Mom says.

"What did you do?" I look at Willow. "Was that storm *yours?*"

Willow at least has the sense to look sheepish. "I didn't think it would work! Other than readings, when has anything I've tried *ever* worked?"

Mom pats her hand soothingly. "There, there, Willow."

Magnolia rolls her eyes. "This is why I stick to good old-fashioned science."

I bury my face in my hands. "Oh my god, *all* of you. Please stop." When silence finally descends, I continue. "Yes, it's Quinton. He showed up right as I was making the potion and we—we fell in love and all I can think is that it's the potion. Because it has to be. And never mind that his family wants the flower for their own perfume." I pull my hands away and look at them. "What do I do?"

They're silent. Then Mom speaks. "Falling in love at first sight is a gift, Clementine. The potion didn't do that."

"But—"

She holds her hand up. "I have an antidote to the potion. You both take it, and if the love really is only because of the potion, then it'll be done. As for his family's desire for the flower, just give him another bottle of the essence."

I gape at her. "What? But you said not to do that!"

"I said you'd know what to do. I assumed, wrongly it appears, that you'd know I meant to give them another full bottle. They'll be able to figure out how to reproduce a scent close enough to it, and they'll be fine."

My cheeks heat as shame floods my gut. "Oh."

She chuckles. "The flower is important to us, obviously, but girls, we're not some crazed women whose entire existence revolves around the flower. And the Henry family isn't made up of villains who want to rob us of something so important."

"Can we go back to the part where Clementine said she was in love?" Magnolia asks, whipping her head to me. "Is it *true*?"

I shrug. "That's what the antidote has to determine."

"Then I'll pull the tea together," Mom says, turning to busy herself behind the bar with dried herbs and flowers and who knows what else.

All I can do is watch, helpless. Will this all be gone in a matter of hours? Or is it possible that maybe, just maybe, there's something real with Quinton? And what does it say about me that for once, I'd like science to be wrong, to fall to its knees in the face of illogical love?

QUINTON

I'M FINISHING A burger and fries in my hotel room when the text comes through.

CLEMENTINE
Can you come to the shop?

The next text is a pin to Rowan's Apothecary & Books. Before I can answer, a third message appears.

CLEMENTINE
And I'll give you a bottle of the essence. For your family.

The tiniest ember of hope begins to flare.

I'll be there. Give me however long it takes to walk there.

CLEMENTINE
I'm sending a rideshare your way.

I didn't think there were any here?

CLEMENTINE

There are.

I don't bother with another text, because it doesn't matter. I toss the to-go box into the trash and throw on my suit pants and dried out shoes, then put on the shirt I'd worn earlier today. I'd really not thought this visit through, because all I have is my suit and three shirts. But I'll deal with that later. For now, I just need to get downstairs.

An SUV pulls up a few minutes later, and the old man driving it grins as I climb into the back. "Seems you're wanted by the Rowan women."

My heart pounds, and my body tingles at the prospect of holding Clementine in my arms again. "Just one. Clementine."

The man smiles and pulls onto the street. "Ah. The baby of the bunch. Sweet girl." He lowers his voice to a whisper. "I like her the best—but don't tell her mama."

I don't quite know what to make of that, so I promise not to say anything. We ride in silence to the shop, and when I try to pay him, he waves me off.

"First ride's on me," he says.

I thank him and climb out, then head inside. Immediately, my eyes find Clementine's and my heart leaps into my throat. She's sitting at what appears to be an old soda fountain, the wooden counter gleaming from years of use, the wall behind her covered with a giant cabinet of various sized drawers. She fights a smile, and her cheeks go pink with a blush that I know is probably on her chest, as well. I make my way to the woman who is everything I have ever wanted.

It's only when I get to her that I bother noticing the women around her. Willow is on one side of Clementine, studying me even more intently than she did this morning, and the teacher from the classroom Clementine was in is on the other. Behind the counter is a woman even smaller than Clementine, and she smiles up at me as she pours four cups of tea.

"Hi," Clementine says, her voice almost shy as I take her hands.

I lean in to brush a kiss on her cheek, catching her particular citrus scent as I do. "Hi, gorgeous."

She clears her throat and straightens, pulling away as she glances at the woman behind the counter. "This is my mom, Daphne. You met Willow this morning, and this is Magnolia."

"Nice to meet you both," I say.

Daphne sets all four cups onto the counter, and nods at Clementine.

"Tea?" Clementine asks, taking one and handing it to me.

I accept, then take a deep inhale to place the ingredients. It's incredibly similar to the love potion, but there's something else in there. Cherry? Whatever it is, it's interesting. I take a sip. "This is very good," I say to Daphne. "Yours?"

Her eyes light up. "Yes. Thank you."

I nod, then take another drink, feeling as though I'm an animal in an exhibit. "So..." I start, completely unsure of what to do next.

And then I feel it.

"Oh," Clementine says, setting the cup down and putting a hand to her stomach. "Oh, no."

"You, too?" I ask, managing to get my own tea on the counter before gripping it to stay upright. "What was in here?" I ask Daphne.

She and Willow don't seem at all affected, but I don't expect them to be. I know exactly what's going on. Gritting my teeth through the nausea roiling through me, I manage, "Whose idea was this?"

"Told you he was smarter than you were giving him credit for," Willow says to her mother.

"Bathroom," Clementine gasps, then slides off the stool and runs to the back.

I follow, and in seconds I'm grabbing the small trash can as Clementine leans over the toilet. For the next few minutes, things aren't great.

"Was this *really* necessary?" I attempt to joke as my stomach seizes. When nothing else comes, I relax against the wall and breathe. "Hell of a way to get to know someone, Sprite. I would have thought going to the bathroom in front of each other came before this."

"Sorry," she says, hands on her knees after flushing again. "But it wasn't my idea."

I laugh. "You are such a liar," I say, gently scooting her out of the way, then emptying and rinsing the trashcan as best as I can before setting it down.

"Caught," she smiles wryly. Then she grabs small paper cups and fills them with water. Next, she doles out mouth-wash. "Why am I not surprised you knew that?"

I raise an eyebrow and tap my chest over my heart. "Because I know you. In here."

She hums, and after another round of water and mouth-wash, we leave the bathroom.

"Does your mother regularly craft teas that make people puke?" I ask, following the sway of her hips as she leads me back to the front.

She gives me another smile. "To be honest? I don't know. Seems they've cleared out."

I look around. The others are indeed gone and the lights are off. Battery-powered candles are still lit throughout the space, giving us just enough to see by. "Cozy," I say, then look back at Clementine as I gesture around. "I think they're on my side."

She studies me closely. "Did it work?"

I grin. "If the idea was to demonstrate the kind of family I'm walking into—the kind that uses tea as a delivery system for love potion antidotes and who knows what else—then yes, it worked." I back her up to the bar and cage her between my arms. "But if you're asking whether the antidote worked, then you'd first have to assume that the love potion worked."

Her brilliant mossy eyes shimmer as I lean closer. "Well?" she asks.

God, she smells so good. I can feel her warmth, the way our bodies strain for each other. There's nothing fake or created about this. It's all so perfectly, incredibly real. Her chest heaves, nearly touching mine as I hover my lips near the sensitive skin beneath her ear. "You know the answer, Clementine."

She shudders. "I do?"

I skim a hand up her arm—the burned one, the beautiful one—and bring it up to the exposed skin of her nape, right where I've learned she's incredibly sensitive. "The answer is I love you. This was going to happen, love potion or not."

"Oh thank god," she lets out, then pulls my lips to hers.

CLEMENTINE

" I LOVE YOU." The words burst out of me without hesitation.

"About fucking time," he murmurs, his eyes crinkling before he kisses me again.

But it feels so good to say it. "I love you." I repeat it again and again between kisses.

Quinton deepens the kiss, silencing me as his body presses to mine. He is my world. No, it doesn't make sense, and yes, there's a little bit of magic in here somewhere, but it doesn't matter. His hands tighten on my waist as he thrusts against me.

"I need you, Clementine," he says against my neck.

I palm his considerable dick and groan, grateful for the angle of the shop windows and the way no one can see us against the counter. "Tell me something," I say as I push his suit jacket off for the second time today. "What do you wear when you're not in a suit?"

He huffs a laugh and helps me with the buttons of his shirt. "Sweatpants and t-shirts at home, jeans, regular clothes."

"And underwear," I say as we rid him of his pants and shoes. "Do you wear it under the sweatpants?"

"Are we really talking about this right now?" He pulls my t-shirt and bra off, then pulls a nipple into his hot mouth.

"Answer the question," I say, my eyes rolling back in my head at the sensation.

"No underwear," he mumbles, then he straightens and reaches up to the pencil out of my hair. "Your hair is a kink all its own, Sprite," he says, his voice deep and gravelly. Then he grips the hair at the back of my head and tilts my chin up. He licks my top lip, then bottom, before tracing the seam.

I shudder, unable to help the mewl that escapes me as I ache for that talented tongue of his to get between my legs.

He hums and tightens his grip on my nape, sending spikes of pleasure streaking through me. "We have a lot to talk about, love, but right now, I'd like to put my mouth on your pussy and make you come. And I'd like to do that without having a whole-ass conversation. Can we do that?"

"Yes," I manage, my mouth dry.

His eyes darken and a decadent smile crosses his lips. "Get naked. I want you on this counter."

Part of me wants to object, because this is my mother's apothecary shop and people use this counter all the time. But the other part, the part that will happily do whatever this man tells me to do, hustles to divest myself of all my clothes.

"Wait," I say, a slow smile spreading. "Get up there."

He stares at me. "I believe I said that I wanted *you* up there, sweetheart."

"Oh, I'll get up there, too. But seeing as how the potion that started this whole thing—"

"It wasn't the potion."

"—was number sixty-nine, I figure we should, I don't know, do something in homage to it."

He chuckles. "I really, *really* can't wait to get to know you better."

I motion him along. "Get your hot ass on the counter and assume the position, Q."

It's not graceful, and I suppress a laugh at the sight of this giant man hauling his naked self up there.

"Oh, you think you're funny," he says, "but you try making it sexy getting up here."

I flip my hair and step onto the stool behind the counter, and I'm up and straddling him in seconds.

He glares playfully at me. "Not fair."

"Never said I was trying to be," I shrug.

He swats my ass lightly. "Turn around and give me that pussy, Clementine."

I lift up and turn around, and as he grabs my hips and lowers me down where he wants me, I help myself to his cock. With every stroke of his tongue against me, I match it with a lick along his length. Before long, I'm taking him to the back of my throat and moaning at the pressure of his tongue against my clit. It's too good. How is he this good? I groan as his tongue sweeps down and around, then I grip the base of his cock, sucking the head and doing my best to match his incredible talent. When I suck hard while scraping my nails along the inside of his thigh, he jerks, nearly coming off the counter.

"Holy fuck, Clementine," he gasps.

"Guess you like that," I say, then do it again.

He groans. "Any more of that and I'm done." He lifts me off him, then gets off the counter as I sit up. "Get over here," he orders, then pulls me to him and has his mouth back between my legs in a heartbeat.

I suck in a breath as his tongue goes right back to my clit. "You are an expert at this," I manage, my legs starting to shake as he pushes a finger into me.

He looks up at me. "I want to be an expert on *you*,

Clementine. Only you." Then he pushes a second finger in and licks, and I whimper.

The feeling is so intense I see stars. "Fuck, Quinton, I love you," I say, my entire body tensing as he thrusts his fingers deep into me.

He doesn't answer, only intensifies his efforts. And as his other hand cradles me in place, I shatter, coming apart so thoroughly that I barely know my name. One hand grips the counter and the other holds his shoulder, and for a moment, it's as if I'm between worlds, suspended between this one and one where angels roam.

I go limp, and before I can recover, he pulls me down, flips me around and stands me on the stool, then presses against me. His cock feels like silk as he rubs it up and down my ass. "Can I have you like this?" he asks against my ear, his voice as deep as the galaxy itself. "Bare?"

I've never let anyone inside me without protection, but for Quinton? Anything. I nod, my core clenching in anticipation.

He rumbles contentedly, then kisses my neck before pushing me down so my chest is against the cool wood of the counter. His hands run down my back, then around to frame my ass. "I was wrong," he says. "It's not just your hair that's a kink. It's your whole fucking body." He massages my ass, then positions himself against me.

I go on to my tiptoes, a silent invitation. "Please, Quinton," I beg. Because never have I needed anything more. Then I'm yelling, a guttural moan of sheer pleasure as he thrusts into me.

"So good, baby," he says, pulling out and pushing in again, getting deeper. "So fucking tight for me—so fucking perfect. You're mine," he grunts against my swiveling hips. "*Fuck*, Clementine. Mine."

I push my hips back, needing every delicious inch he's

giving me and meeting him with every movement. "Yours," I say. He fucks me like we have all the time in the world, decadently, slowly, sliding in and out of me with a luxuriousness that I have never known. Then he reaches around to my clit and I'm on the precipice again.

"You gonna let me come inside you?" he asks, lifting me up and sweeping my hair to the side before leaning me back against his chest. Then he presses a hand against my breast and captures a nipple between his fingers, sending a ripple of pleasure straight to my pussy.

"Anything you want, Quinton," I say, nearly delirious with pleasure.

"Fall apart for me," he urges. "I've got you. Let go."

He thrusts again, harder than before, nearly lifting me entirely off the stool. I shout, and I swear lightning surges through me, the same jolt from our initial touch in the greenhouse but magnified, reaching from my head to my fingertips and toes before curling back and burying itself deep inside me.

I can't speak, can only gasp as he murmurs, "I know. Me, too," and then we're both toppling into our orgasms in a bliss so complete it leaves me speechless.

Spent, his lips find my neck again as he holds me tight, our arms threaded between each other around my waist. For a long moment, all we do is breathe.

Finally, I turn around in his embrace. His eyes are gentle and sweet in the dim light, full of a world I can't wait to explore. "Stay here," I say. "With me."

He grins. "Of course."

My heart soars. "Really?"

He laughs softly. "It's going to require some logistics, but yeah, Sprite, I'm staying."

I pull his mouth to mine and lose myself in him all over again.

EPILOGUE

THREE MONTHS LATER

"There they are, the perfume prince of Canada and his beautiful bride to be!"

I scowl at Magnolia as I throw my bag into the back seat of her car. "You're hilarious."

She laughs. "I mean, it's true."

I blow a raspberry at her and scramble into the back as she says, "Get in before I leave you two here to find your own way home."

My butt hits the back seat and I swat at her. "What does it look like we're doing?"

"I can't believe I'm marrying into this," Quinton mutters as he accordions himself into the tiny Fiat.

I swat at him, too, and he barely closes the door before Magnolia punches the gas, making the wheels chirp and sending the dream catcher hanging from her rear-view mirror swinging. "Good lord, Mags, what's the rush?"

"I have plans," she says haughtily, "and this hour-long drive is really putting me in a pinch."

I look closer at her. "It's Thursday afternoon and school's out. You never have plans. Wait. Are you…are you wearing *make-up?*"

"Shut up," she says, then plops an oversize pair of sunglasses off her head and onto her nose.

I hum, trying to figure her out. "It's a guy," I pronounce.

The Fiat swerves, and Quinton grips the door so tightly his knuckles lighten. "Sweetie, could you maybe not tease your sister when we're in this death trap?" he asks, his voice pitching up.

"Agreed," Magnolia sniffs.

"Fine, but I'm getting the story out of you later," I say, crossing my arms.

An hour later, Mags drops us off at our new place. Well, not new. The tiny cabin sits at the edge of our land and is where my great-grandmother used to live. I've always loved it, but it's a bit, shall we say, rustic. The first time Quinton walked inside, he immediately backed out and called the local builder to get an "actual house that actual people in the actual twenty-first century live in" built. And it turns out that Quinton is straight-up loaded, so progress on the house has been swift.

Honestly, the entire past three months have been swift. A few days after the Great Counter Experience—as I'm choosing to call it—Quinton whisked me up to Coal's Lake to meet his family, who didn't blink at him bringing an American home. And that was before I held up the bottle of Elysian Blossom essence. After that, it was hugs and celebrations all around. It took a month, but I helped Quinton and the perfumists figure out how to duplicate the essence in a lab to finalize the anniversary scent. I also met his friends, had sex all over his apartment, and got engaged. Then it was back home for an extended stay, and back up to Coal's Lake for the past few weeks to pack up Quinton's apartment and ready his stuff to be shipped to Sacred River.

I've barely set my bags down before Quinton's grabbing my hand and tugging me back outside, a secretive smile on his face.

"What is it?" I ask, unable to keep from smiling right back at him. Then I see where he's taking me. The willow tree.

He leads me through the wisps of leaves and takes us to the trunk. It's peaceful in here, the cool of the tree's shade a relief against the May sun. Cardinals chirp above me, and I know it's the same pair that whistled to me the morning I first met my love.

Looking up, I spy the male's red form and whistle back at him and his mate. Quinton leans against the tree, gathers me into his arms and kisses me, taking his time exploring my mouth, languid and lush. It's my favorite kind of Quinton kiss, unless you count the demanding, drugging kisses I get when he's pushing into me, his body taking mine to heights I never knew existed. I breathe in the wintry pine scent of him and his thumb grazes my cheek as I fist his shirt, going onto my tiptoes for more. Later, we'll undress and feast on each other as the sun sets, sending its orange rays through the gauzy curtains. But for now, I have everything I could ever want.

"I love you so much, Clementine," he says, leaning his forehead to mine.

I smile up at him. "I love you, too."

WANT MORE? Keep going for a sneak peak at Book Two in the Sacred River series!

Karaoke Chemistry

Magnolia

I make it to the parking lot with five minutes to spare. Pulling into a partially-hidden space, I kill the engine and reach into the back seat for my tote. It's a familiar routine at this point, throwing on the black tee with a glitter skull over my pink tank top and wiggling into ripped black jeans. I slide off the muted cotton skirt and open my make-up kit, lining my eyes in the visor mirror with a royal blue glitter eyeliner, then smudging it in. After fluffing my hair, I get out and go to the back of my Fiat to step into the black Doc Martens that only get worn here. I lock my car, hustle to the door, then take a deep breath before wrenching it open and making a straight line through the crowd for the emcee bent over tonight's list.

Carol straightens as I near, then smiles at me in delight. "Seven! I didn't think you'd make it tonight."

I start to apologize, but remember that Seven doesn't say sorry. Ever. So I stand tall and shrug like it's no big deal. "Hi Carol. Had some things to do today. You know how it goes."

She hands me the pen and my silver bracelets clink against each other as I write my name and song selections down. I'm feeling extra sassy after dealing with my sister and her fiancé earlier, so I choose Joan Jett's "I Love Rock 'n' Roll" and No Doubt's "Just a Girl," two fun songs that I can easily lose myself in and forget the rest of the world. I'm last on the list, but Carol likes me—or at least the twenties I give her every time I sing—so I know I'll get on stage at least once tonight.

I hand the pen back with a smile and make my way to the bar to order Seven's usual drink: a high-end whiskey, neat, water on the side. It is definitely *not* what the real me would order, but when I'm at Al's, I'm not Magnolia Rowan, quiet high school chemistry teacher and least-interesting of the many Rowan sisters. Here, I'm Seven, bad-ass singer who doesn't care what anyone thinks. Here, I flirt with the bartender even though he looks like he's barely old enough to drink, let alone serve alcohol. Here, I'm a woman who takes what she wants. Who is unapologetically herself. Who has a powerhouse voice, literally *and* metaphorically, and isn't afraid to use it.

In other words, the exact opposite of who I really am.

"Wondered if you'd be here tonight," a deep voice says.

He's here. Magnolia would never be so bold, but as Seven, I turn and let my eyes travel from his boots up his jeans-clad legs to a trim waist, up a black Henley that hugs a thick chest and arms, on up to a jaw covered in dark gray and silver stubble, and finally up to bright blue eyes that crinkle deliciously as he smiles at me. My belly tightens in response.

"Riggs."

He clinks his beer against my whiskey. "Seven."

"You miss me?" I tease.

"All week," he answers. "You?"

"Obviously." I glance away and take another sip, unable to hold his stare. There's only so much of Seven that really works in the face of this man's self-assured presence. I've seen him here almost every week for at least a year, and every time, it's the same: a little bit of flirting and nothing more. I don't know his last name and he doesn't know my real name. For all I know, he's hiding who he is just as much as I am.

We turn our attention to Carol, who's kicking the evening into gear with the opening verse of "Shake it Off." I lean against the bar and try not to shrink under Riggs' assessing gaze, fighting the instinct to curl into myself as I take another sip of the whiskey, letting its burn fortify me. "What are you singing?" I ask, keeping my eyes on Carol.

He shifts beside me. "Why? You want to duet?"

I scoff. "You can't handle me."

"That remains to be seen," he says quietly.

Goosebumps skitter across my skin at the thought of giving myself over to him. His broad body hovering over mine, the scruff of his insanely-hot stubble against my neck as he lowers himself down, the way that scruff might feel in other places. I suppress a moan and take another sip, thankful for the dim light. I need to slow down on the drink.

"Africa," he says.

"That's your song?"

He nods, and as he tips back his beer I take the two-second opportunity to study him. His closely-cropped hair fades into longer strands on top, the perfect length for grabbing onto. The man is the very definition of silver fox, and carries himself in a way that communicates he's used to getting his way. Outside of this bar—outside of being Seven —I'd never have the courage to speak to him. Even still, I feel every bit of the sheltered school teacher when I'm next to him, and no matter how hard I try, I'm never on solid ground when he's this close.

Carol finishes the song and calls Riggs up. He looks over at me and winks. "Wish me luck."

I smirk. "You need nothing of the sort."

He puts his hands in his pockets as he backs away, the move serving only to highlight the broadness of his chest and arms. The man is a tank. What I'd give to be run over by him. "I need whatever you want to give me," he says, then pivots away.

My mouth dries.

He saunters to Carol and takes the mic from her hands with a smile, then turns to address the crowd of about fifty. "I'm going to need some backup from you guys on this one— are you ready?" The crowd cheers back, its pleasure increasing as the first memorable notes flow out of the speakers.

I know that Riggs can't see me from his vantage point on the tiny stage, but that knowledge doesn't stop the tightness in my chest when he looks my way and sings. Seven would give that energy right back to Riggs, so I polish off the whiskey and make my way to the front of the crowd just in time for the chorus. And when our eyes lock and the butter-flies in my stomach erupt, I let them take flight, reveling in the escape from real life for just a little while.

~~~~~~~~~~~

Also by Valerie Pepper

Guided to Love Series

The Mechanic's Guide to Getting the Boss's Daughter (series starter novella)

The Widow's Guide to Second Chances (Book 1)

The Barista's Guide to The Perfect Steam (Book 2)

The Grump's Guide to Chaos (Book 3)

Sacred River Series

Love Potion No. 69 (Book 1 - Series starter novella)

Karaoke Chemistry (Book 2 - coming Summer 2024)

Beale Street Blues Series

Love, On the Rocks (Book 1 - 2024)

Novellas

Naughty All The Way (November 2023) - Part of the Twelve Days of Smutmas limited-time collection

To Have and To Scold in the *Holidays & Hook-Ups* anthology by The New Romance Cafe (June 2023 - limited edition)

Acknowledgments

This one is for the readers, the Bookstagrammers, the Booktokkers, the reviewers, and the ARC readers: Thank you, thank you, thank you. Thank you for the love you continue to show me and my books. Thank you for giving me your time, your enthusiasm, your memes, your exclamation points, grabby hands, and hearts. It means so much to me.

    xo,

Valerie Pepper

About the Author

 Valerie Pepper is an incurable optimist and a firm believer in the girl getting the guy, or the guy getting the girl, or the girl getting the girl, or the guy getting the guy, or basically any way it needs to happen to make a real-life happily ever after, even if it takes more than one try.

When she's not writing, you can find her reading, hiking, listening to whatever music suits her mood, and hanging out with her family. She's fascinated with the idea of a capsule wardrobe, but loves clothes and shoes and boots far too much to make a real go of it.

She's currently living out her own happily ever after with her husband, kids, and dogs, and maaaaaybe too many shoes. She lives in Birmingham, Alabama, and is the recipient of the Contemporary Romance Writer's 2021 Stiletto Award. Learn more at www.authorvaleriepepper.com.

Printed in Great Britain
by Amazon

43897524R00066